Parent's Introduction

Whether your child is a beginning reader, a reluctant reader, or an eager reader, this book offers a fun and easy way to encourage and help your child in reading.

Developed with reading education specialists, **We Both Read** books invite you and your child to take turns reading aloud. You read the left-hand pages of the book, and your child reads the right-hand pages—which have been written at one of six early reading levels. The result is a wonderful new reading experience and faster reading development!

You may find it helpful to read the entire book aloud yourself the first time, then invite your child to participate the second time. As you read, try to make the story come alive by reading with expression. This will help to model good fluency. It will also be helpful to stop at various points to discuss what you are reading. This will help increase your child's understanding of what is being read.

In some books, a few challenging words are introduced in the parent's text, distinguished with **bold** lettering. Pointing out and discussing these words can help to build your child's reading vocabulary. If your child is a beginning reader, it may be helpful to run a finger under the text as each of you reads. Please also notice that a "talking parent" ⊚ icon precedes the parent's text, and a "talking child" ⊚ icon precedes the child's text.

If your child struggles with a word, you can encourage "sounding it out," but keep in mind that not all words can be sounded out. Your child might pick up clues about a word from the picture, other words in the sentence, or any rhyming patterns. If your child struggles with a word for more than five seconds, it is usually best to simply say the word.

Most of all, remember to praise your child's efforts and keep the reading fun. After you have finished the book, ask a few questions and discuss what you have read together. Rereading this book multiple times may also be helpful for your child.

Try to keep the tips above in mind as you read together, but don't worry about doing everything right. Simply sharing the enjoyment of reading together will increase your child's reading skills and help to start your child off on a lifetime of reading enjoyment!

The Three Little Pigs

A We Both Read® Book: Level K–1
Guided Reading: Level C

_____

Second Edition

Text Copyright © 2017, 1998 by Treasure Bay, Inc.
Illustrations Copyright ©1998 by Erin Marie Mauterer
All rights reserved

We Both Read® is a trademark of Treasure Bay, Inc.

Published by Treasure Bay, Inc.
P.O. Box 119
Novato, CA 94948 USA

Printed in Malaysia

Library of Congress Catalog Card Number: 98-60703

ISBN: 978-1-891327-09-4

Visit us online at:
www.WeBothRead.com

PR-11-17

WE BOTH READ®

The Three Little Pigs

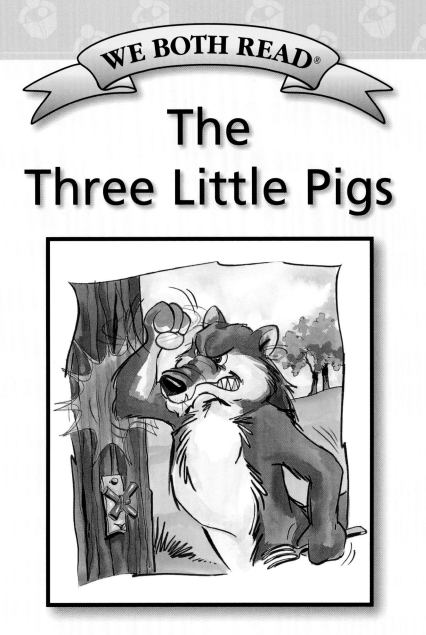

Adapted by Dev Ross

Illustrated by Erin Marie Mauterer

TREASURE **BAY**

There once was a mother pig with so many little pigs that they were always under one foot or another. So one day she said to the three oldest, "**You** must go and make your own way in the world now."

They asked if they could stay, but she said,

"No, no, no!
You must go!"

Now the three little pigs each needed a home, but building a house was a lot of work! The first little pig would much rather watch TV. So when he found some hay, it made him very **happy**.

He said, "A house of hay!

Oh, **happy** day!"

The first little pig built his house as fast as he could. When he was done, he felt he had earned a **rest**. So he turned on his TV and said with a sigh,

"I will just sit
and **rest** a bit."

Nearby, a wolf was watching. Now, this was not a nice wolf. This was a very bad wolf.

The wolf knocked on the door, but the **little** pig's TV was too loud for the **little** pig to hear the knocking. So the wolf had to shout,

"**Little** pig,
little pig,
let me in!"

This the little pig could hear!

He did not want to let the wolf in, so he shouted back, "Not by the hair on my chinny chin chin."

The wolf frowned.

He was bad,
and he was mad.

The wolf shouted back, "Then I'll huff and I'll puff and I'll blow your house down."

The wolf took a big breath and blew that straw house down, and the little pig cried,

"Oh no! Oh no!
I must go!"

The first little pig ran away as fast as he could! However, when he realized he'd forgotten his TV, he ran back to get it and the wolf gobbled him up.

"Yummy," said the wolf.

 "Yum, yum, **yummy** in my big, big, tummy!"

The second little pig did not want to build a house either. He would much rather eat. So when he stumbled upon a pile of sticks, it made him very happy.

He said, "A house of sticks . . .

 . . . will be my pick."

The second little pig built his house as fast as he could. When he was done, he felt he deserved to **eat** some treats. So he opened his refrigerator and said with glee, "All these treats . . .

 . . . I will **eat.**"

 Nearby, the wolf was watching.

Up to the door he leaped and knocked loudly. The second little pig, however, was too busy eating to hear, so the wolf had to shout,

"Little pig,
little pig,
let me in!"

 *This* the little pig could hear.

He did not want to let the wolf in. With his mouth full, he shouted back, "Not by the hair on my chinny chin chin."

The wolf scowled.

 He was bad,
and he was mad!

The wolf shouted, "Then I'll huff and I'll puff and I'll blow your house down!"

The wolf took a big breath and blew that house of sticks down, and the little pig cried,

"Oh no! Oh no!
I must go!"

The second little pig ran away as fast as he could. However, when he ran back to get his favorite sucker, the wolf gobbled him up.

"Yummy," said the wolf.

"Yum, yum, yummy
in my big, big, tummy!"

The third little pig also wanted to build a house. So when he found a pile of bricks, it made him very happy.

He said, "A house built well . . .

. . . will be so swell."

The third little pig built his house carefully. Then he washed his dishes and swept the floor.

When he **was** finished, he looked around and said, "**That**'s all done.

 **That was** fun!"

 Nearby, the wolf was watching.

Up to the door he marched and knocked loudly. The third little pig, however, was too smart to answer, so the wolf had to shout,

 "Little pig,
little pig,
let me in!"

This the little pig most certainly heard.

He checked every lock to be sure the wolf couldn't break in before he shouted back, "Not by the hair on my chinny chin chin."

The wolf glared angrily at the big, sturdy door.

He was bad
and he was mad!

The wolf yelled, "Then I'll huff and I'll puff and I'll blow your house down!"

The wolf huffed and he puffed. He puffed and he huffed, but he could not blow that brick house down. He said, "This house of brick . . .

 . . . is much too thick!"

The wolf stopped huffing and puffing
and tried getting in through the chimney
instead.

That was not a good idea.

See the pot?
It is hot!

The wolf landed in the big hot pot, where he turned into a delicious soup. The third little pig gobbled him up. And how did the bad wolf taste?

Not bad!
Not bad!

If you liked **The Three Little Pigs** here are some other
We Both Read® books you are sure to enjoy!

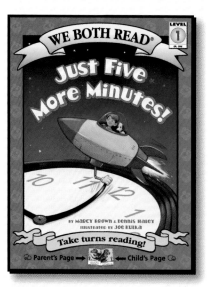

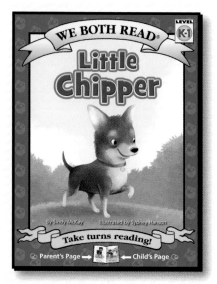

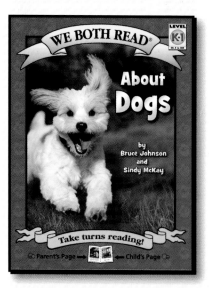

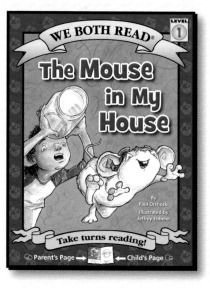

To see all the We Both Read books that are available,
just go online to **www.WeBothRead.com**.